BABY TEETH

a novel in verse

MEG GREHAN

Little Island
Books create waves

BABY TEETH

First published in 2021 by
Little Island Books
7 Kenilworth Park
Dublin 6W
Ireland

A British Library Cataloguing in Publication record for this book
is available from the British Library.

Cover illustration by Ana Jarén
Cover hand lettering by Holly Pereira
Typeset by Kieran Nolan
Proofread by Emma Dunne
Printed in the UK by CPI

Print ISBN: 978-1-912417-90-2

Little Island has received funding to support
this book from the Arts Council of Ireland/An Chomhairle Ealaíon

10 9 8 7 6 5 4 3 2 1

To Weezy
for your endlessly inspiring friendship and kindness

One

There's a specific type of
Shame
I think
That comes with realising
Exactly how little
You understand yourself
It tastes different
Sits heavier on the tongue
It's
It's embarrassing
One little life to figure out

One little self
But

For us
It's sitting at a piano
And playing
Note for note
    With a deftness belonging to someone
    You've never met

But who knows you so deeply
A song
You've never heard

Sliding a book
Old and worn and unfamiliar
From a dusty shelf
And hearing the final words
Whispered in your head
Knowing that
This story
You know
You've never read
Lives in you
Somewhere

Stopping at a painting
Silent and restored
On a museum wall
And feeling a prickle
Behind your eyelids
Telling you
This isn't the first time
You've seen it
Because last time
When the paint still gleamed wetly in the sunshine
It moved you
To tears

Trying new things
And feeling that gentle surge
Of familiarity
Feeling my fingers
Prickle with
Yes
I know this
Yes
I can do this
Yes
I have done this

But I haven't
I haven't done this
I haven't done that
I haven't done anything
That these fingers haven't done before

It's choosing
Over and over
Whether or not
To play the song
To read the book
To study the painting
Because this time
Now that you are you
Does it
Can it

Mean anything
Really

And will it get worse
Each time
The next time
The next life
The next you
Will they feel this
Even more
Even more
Profoundly
Distinctly
Will they feel
With such certainty
That they
Are nothing new
That really
They are nothing
At all

Is that all
You will give them

Is that all
I will give them

Two

This time
I am Immy
Usually
I think
I would know
What that means
By now

My boots don't fit right
They rub my toes wrong
The leather still refusing to give in and
Be mine

But they're keeping the rain out
And they make me feel tall
And I think I was meant to be tall
So I walk like my toes don't hurt

I found my bag under the bed
Wedged in a corner
Missed in the clear out
I shouldn't have it

It shouldn't be mine
Anymore
But the strap is already worn
Right where I like to rub my thumb over it
When I'm nervous
So I dyed it
Beige to black
So the others wouldn't recognise it
And I said I found it
In a charity shop
And maybe an eyebrow
flicked up in recognition
But I wasn't looking

It's cold in the flower shop
It smells of petal and root and dirt
It's cold and it smells like the ground and it welcomes
    me in the way the ground will not
And I like it
I like it
It's cosy
It feels
Nice
It feels
safe

I touch petals and stems
I like the red flowers

They remind me of Freddie
I like the orange ones
They remind me of Henry
I'm not sure which would remind someone
Of me
I wonder if maybe
I'm the bits under the ground
In the dark
The bits that hide
The bits that burrow

I pick up a yellow rose
And hear the words

"That one suits you"

And I turn
I turn
And there
There
Is a girl

I thank her
Because it's a beautiful flower
And I hope that
Thank you
Is the right thing to say

She looks at me
And I look at her
And we look at each other
And something happens
I don't know what
But I know
When I look back
This moment
Looking at her
Will be the moment
When it happened
Whatever it
Is
It happened here
It happened with her

She's cute
She's very
Cute
Her dress long and loose
Her eyes hazel and warm
Warm and intense
Intense and
Cute
She's cute

I ask for flowers
A bouquet
Yellow red orange
        Fire flame flicker
She nods and turns
She picks them carefully
From pots lined up
Covering the wall
She wraps them up
In brown paper
She asks who they're for

I lie and say my father
Because I don't know what else to say
What else to call him

She smiles and says
"Not a girlfriend?"
And I blush
Shake my head
Try to hold eye contact
Fail
Gulp
Try again

She smiles at me
I think I smile back
I mutter that I don't have a girlfriend
Then I worry that I sound like the idea
Of having one

Doesn't sound good
Right
To me
So I scramble
I blurt
Not that I don't want one
Fast
Too fast
Loud
Too loud
And she smiles
And I smile
And I come back a few days later
And a few days later
And soon the house
Is full of flowers
And Freddie is
"Begging, Immy, I am begging"
Me to ask her out
But I don't
I won't
I can't

I do

I arrive as the shop is closing
And she smiles

And she waves
And she mouths
Wait
And I wait
Of course
I wait

It's raining
It's raining
Like it knows
And I think about how
Walking home in the rain
With either
A yes
Or a no
Clutched in my hand
Burning on my tongue
Sitting in my chest
Will feel
Dramatic
either way

Either way

When she comes out
She looks like everything I'd ever wanted
All the different people I'd made up for myself

All the lives and pasts and futures and versions versions
    versions
Carried around in my head my chest my bones my eyelids
She looks like them all
All at once
She looked like everything
I could ever want
Standing in front of me
With dark eyes
And nervous fingertips
Poking shyly from beneath her too-long sleeves
Her boots
Already wet from the rain
Rolling slowly back and forth
Toe to heel and back again
Her lips
Set in a sharp line
She shook and swayed and moved in only the tiniest ways
Imperceptible
A leaf on a windless day
Still moving
But still
She is still
She stands so
Sure
She makes
No sense
To me
Really
She is

Too much
Too good
Too nice
Too
Much
But I feel
For a second
With a certainty I could never voice
That I know her
Entirely
already
So I open my mouth
And I ask
And then I walk home
A yes
A yes that came with a smile and a hug and a Saturday
    morning
Safe in my hand
Warm on my tongue
Nestled in my chest

Freddie is delighted
Henry is concerned

As expected
As expected

Saturday
Takes its time
I try on outfits
Twirl in front of the mirror
Like a girl in a movie
Even if the mirror
Can only show me shadows

Saturday
Arrives
And brings the sun with it
I wear a dress
To feel
Special
And I worry
Up until the second I see her
In a long skirt
A loose top
Glowing
Sunlight dancing over her skin
And I breathe
And I breathe
And I bite my lip
And when she reaches me
I say
Hi
And I smile
And she says

Hi
And she smiles
And it all
All of it
All of this
Begins
Just like that

She sips coffee
I gulp tea
She laughs
I stammer
I blush
I snort when I try to laugh
She smiles
Even brighter

She tells me about her family
The aunt she lives with
Who owns the flower shop
She tells me about working there
About colour and dirt and thorn
About art
About paint and brush and charcoal
About herself
About softness and light and secrets

We laugh and we talk and we talk and we laugh
And we are together
So together
And it's easy
So soon
It's easy
And I wonder
What I was ever
Nervous about

Three

Henry always buys pants
A couple inches
Too short
Some lingering habit
Ghosts in his bones
We think

"I can't be that tall though"
He says
As he folds them neatly
With all the rest
"Let us buy them next time"
We say
But he never does
Just keeps living
The tiniest bit
in the tiniest way
In a body
Long gone

It's funny
What stays
Filmy and slippery
Elusive

But stubborn
Just loud enough
To always be heard
When it wants to be
To always make sure
Henry has slightly chilly ankles

We buy him socks a lot
Every time we see a pair
With especially bright colours
Or especially cute designs
Or especially silly puns
We try to out-do each other
Find the most garish or the most adorable
the most ridiculous
And he always wears them
Proudly on display beneath his too-short pants
With his perfectly ironed button-ups
And his shiny shoes

We don't have a lot of stuff
We start over
Clean
Every time
When one of us Goes
The others

Shake out their existence
Dust it all off
Box it all up
Give it all away
Spread it all out
We're all over the city
We're in charity shop basements
Strangers' attics
Dumps and museums
We box our friends up
And we give them away
And we wait for them to come back
And we start over again

We die
We start again
We die
We start again
We find each other
We haunt each other
We hold each other
We forget
We forget
We try not to mourn the ones we lose
We try to love the ones we have
We die
We start again
We find

We haunt
We hold

I wonder who I've been
What I've been
What I've done
I wonder if the small voice
That reaches for every piano
Broke someone's heart
If the deep voice that shies away from red things
Hurt someone
If the airy voice that hates the rain
Killed someone
I wonder what these bones have done
I wonder what I carry
I wonder who I am

History
Feels
Like possibilities
The vampire in the castle
The madman in the trees
The head on the stake
Or in the basket
The witch by the sea
The woman in the lake
The boy in the boat

The
The
The
Were they me
Are they me
Did they carry these bones
Are they beneath this skin

I wonder
How much of me
They make up
How much of me
I can claim
How much
I want to

I try to be good
I promise
I do
I don't cause pain
I try
I don't hurt
I try

I am polite
Please and thank you
Excuse me and bless you

I am polite
I try
I promise
I try
I try to make up for it all
I don't know
Exactly
What I need to make up for
What I need to amend
So I try
I try
To fix it all
Make up for it all
Make amends
Make amends
Make amends

Freddie says it's
Stupid
He says
I am me   you are you
I am only me   you are only you
And I'm only responsible   you are only responsible
For what I do   what you do
What I've done   what you've done
What I will do   what you will do
Freddie says

Henry doesn't say anything
I think maybe Henry
Understands
Maybe Henry
Gets it
But Henry has been Henry
Much longer than I have been Immy
So maybe Henry
Has less to make up for

I think Freddie
Probably understands too
I think Freddie
Just doesn't want to

Freddie is only a little older than me
This time
He's been Freddie
For twenty-three years
And I've known him
For most of them

Freddie cooks
It's his
Thing
He says

Freddie likes control
So Freddie
Says who he is
What he is
What he does
He decides
He decided
So
Freddie cooks

Freddie is not good at cooking
But we still eat his food
I suppose
That's who we've decided to be
People who love
Freddie
And all of his stupid
Decisions

Freddie says
I should stop worrying
He says he likes who I am
A pretty okay little sister
A pretty good friend
A pretty great
A pretty great

Freddie says I should stop worrying

Henry likes flowers and cleanliness
He is the opposite of Freddie
And possibly
The very same as me
It's hard to tell
All I know for certain about Henry
Is that he loves us
Deeply
And when needs be
Aggressively
Henry has been Henry for a long time
I don't know how long
Neither does Freddie
But I think
We've been the young ones
More than once
With Henry

I wonder sometimes
How loud it is in his head
Henry
How heavy he feels
How much he remembers
I wonder

But I know he won't tell
Maybe it's been so long
He can quieten them
Maybe it's been so long
They gave up

We have lived
So many lifetimes
Been so many people
We've been
So much
We've done
So much
And it's all stored up
Inside us
All of them
All the selves we've
Been
They're in there
In here
In me
In each of us
They are there
And they are loud
They miss their lives
Henry told me
They miss control
And so they try

They try to tell
They try to command
They try and they try
They are sad
They are stuck
They had their turns
I tell them
You had your turn
They had their turns
And if they wasted them
If they didn't do
All they wanted
there's nothing I can do
now
to help them
I tell them
I try

I wonder if next time
After this time
Ends
If that one
The new one
The one who carries me in their bones
In their blood
I wonder
If they'll hear me
I wonder

What I'll reach for
What I'll surge forward to see
What I'll miss
Who I'll scream for
I wonder
Will I make their life
unbearable
Or will I fade away
Sink back
Into a corner of their mind
Will I be
Will I be

I wonder what they'll be like
The next one
Will they be a girl
A boy
Neither
Both
Will it matter
To them
Who they are
Will they be
Loud
Will they fizz with life
Will they be clever
Will they change the world
Will they be good

Will they be good
They are me
As I am them
　　　As we all are
　　　　　　This line
　　　　　　This collection
　　　　　　This self and self and self

　　　　　　We are
　　　　　　One
　　　　　　Aren't we
　　　　　　I'm just a part
　　　　　　Aren't I
　　　　　　Just a piece
　　　　　　A whole lifetime
　　　　　　Is just another
　　　　　　Moment
　　　　　　Isn't it
　　　　　　We are us
　　　　　　They are me
　　　　　　I am
　　　　　　I am

I am

I hope I am good

I've read about others
Old ones
Who impaled
Who terrorised
Who bit and drained and took
Who took and took and took
Who killed and killed and killed
And I
And I

I hope I am good

I think Henry is good
Freddie too
I think they are good
But I only know them
As they are
And I forget the rest
The ones inside might know
Otherwise
But I will not listen
and they do not tell

Their voices aren't clear
They are too fast

Too slow
Too loud too quiet
Sometimes they sob
Sometimes they moan
Sometimes
They scream together
One big voice
Deep
Settled in the back of my skull
Like the feeling of being watched
The feeling of being followed
They form a mass
A clump
A cluster
And they talk and they talk and they talk
An amalgamation of want and need and sorrow and loss
    and fear and anger
Of jealousy and regret
Of hatred and pity and
I can't understand their words
Too fast
Too many
Too much
I can't understand
Their words
But I understand their
Feelings
I understand
What they want me to know
That they are stuck
And I will be too

I walk a lot
to drown them out
When they are loud
To keep them quiet
When they aren't

I walk through the house
I walk through the city
I walk through life
Eyes down
Bones heavy
I walk

Freddie says
I need to make friends
And that
Maybe
A hobby
Wouldn't hurt

His apron is covered in splatters
Usually grey
It's all the colours of a garden now
And the pot on the hob
Is spitting
Like it's joining the conversation
The kitchen is chaos
The kitchen is always chaos

But after we've filled our stomachs
Henry will swoop in
And everything will gleam
As always
They fit
Freddie and Henry
As always

We eat
Food
Of course
We need it
Our bodies need it

The blood
It isn't for our bodies
The blood is for our
Minds
For our selves
For our pasts
For quiet
The blood
Feeds the hunger
That threatens everything
The blood
It keeps us
Us
But I can't ever seem

To get enough
I can't ever seem
To get a firm enough grasp
To keep myself
Myself
To get a good look
To know
For sure

In the mornings
I try to ignore myself
I try to start a day
Without noticing
Whatever is asking to be noticed
If I am sad
I ignore it
If I am fuzzy
I ignore it
If I am thrumming with energy
Ignore it
If I am someone else entirely
Ignore it
It never works
Never helps
But I ignore that too

I tried to break the rule
A couple times
We don't ask
That's the rule
We don't ask about ourselves
Don't ask to claim our own histories
If we remember
Then we remember
But secrets stay secrets
But I tried
This time
This time is different
I insisted
This time feels different
And Henry gave me a *look*
And asked how I could possibly know that
And I gave him a *look*
And said
I just do
I just know
This time is different
I'm not anyone
This time
I'm not anything
This time
And they both looked at me
And at each other
And sighed
And said no
No no no
And I cried

And I tried
To explain
To make it make sense
Or to show them
How little sense
it made
But they just held me
And shushed me
And I chanted
Over and over
I don't know
I don't know
I don't know
Until it all stopped
Until I was empty
Until
For a moment
I was so tired
That I just
Didn't care
Anymore
And I wished them
Goodnight
And ignored the look they shared
And went to bed

We only tell each other
Histories

If we absolutely must
And it's not like we have
That many
We can still remember
But even when
We forget ourselves
Somehow
We hold on a little tighter
To each other
I know more about them
Than I know about myself
And sometimes
That terrifies me
And sometimes
I'm just glad I know
Something

It was easier
The last few years
Because we could put it all down
No matter how irrationally
To my being a teenager
As it turns out
No matter how many times you live it
Puberty
Can still feel like it's ripping the life out of you
But each year
While I settled

While I grew
The panic grew too
The unease
The discomfort
The voice chanting
This isn't right

Is the body even mine
Has any body ever
Really
Been mine

The first
Maybe
The original
But I remember
Nothing of it
Its shape its colour its make up
Maybe
I think
That was me
The purest
Realest me
And everything since then
Is pretend
Is costume
Is disguise
Is untrue

But
Try as I might
I can't remember that first body
That first self
Sometimes
I feel
With a stubborn and unearned certainty
That I was a boy
That I was a man
But other times
I know
Though I cannot know
That no
I was a woman
I know that since
I've been both
One at a time
Or both at once or
Sometimes
Neither
And maybe
I think
Some nights
It doesn't matter
What I was
At the start
But still
Still
It would be nice to know
It would be nice to know

Four

She smells like paint
Just a little
And peppermint tea
Warm and cold
Comforting and refreshing
She has long fingers
That never stop moving
And just one dimple
Nestled in her left cheek
Messy eyebrows and freckles
But only if you look closely
She leans to the side
More often than not
Because she carries too much with her
But refuses to use anything
Other than that one beaten leather bag
Hooked over one shoulder
She always has extra hair ties
And painkillers
Tampons and tissues
Lip balm
A pen
She's always ready
For her own just-in-case
or anyone else's
She will ask the crying stranger if they need help

She will cross the street to pet the dog
She will share her umbrella
She smells like paint and peppermint tea and her hand
    will hold yours with the perfect balance of strength
    and tenderness and she will say your name when she
    doesn't have to because she wants you to know she
    sees you and she's listening and she cares about what
    you say and she will give you the last piece of gum
    and she will say the tough thing when she knows it's
    the right thing and she will forget the name of the
    book but remember that they kissed for the first time
    on page 136 but fell in love on page 47 she's sure of it
    and she will remember your coffee order and she will
    compliment you only when she means it so you never
    need to question that yes yes your hair looks lovely
    and you have kind eyes and you make people happy
    and in all of my lives and in all of my selves I have
    never and could never and will never be deserving of
Her

On a Thursday
She gives me a rose

Yellow

And I hold it
Like it could break

I feel the pad of my thumb
Pressing on a
Thorn
Pressing
Like I could break
If I chose to
If I tried
Hard enough

We kiss goodbye at her door
And I carry the rose home

Yellow

And into the kitchen
And I put it in a glass
And I feed it
Water
And I think about how
It's the most
Alive
Thing in
This house

And how it came from her
And how
Of course
It came from her

The rose lives on the kitchen table
Right in the middle
And I think
Maybe I'm supposed to keep it in my room
Look to it each night before I sleep
Like it represents
Her

But it does
Represent her

So I keep it in the kitchen
Where everyone can see it

The rose
Yellow

Where everyone can see it
And say
Oh
Look at this
Where did this come from
Isn't it
Lovely

And it will stand out
Bright and fresh and

Yellow

And good

And it makes us all
Smile
When we see it
we think
Claudia

Claudia
Has a green thumb
Green fingers
Green palms and green wrists
Dirt beneath her fingernails
The smell of outside
Following her
Fresh and alive
Fresh and alive

Claudia
Wears her hair in a plait
Down her back
She ties it with a ribbon
Or string
Or elastic
Whatever she can find
I like the ribbon
It soothes a part of me I don't recognise
Calms some old self
Makes them feel at home
I give her ribbons sometimes

Saying oh
I found this
Isn't it nice
Like that dusty, lonely self
Hadn't put its palm over mine
Gripped my fingers with a tired desperation
Old bones begging
And snatched up the ribbons
And the coins in my pocket
And marched me to the till

They do look pretty
Lopsided little bows
Loosening throughout the day
Until the ribbon falls like a leaf
To the ground
And wisps of dark hair
Flutter around her face
And this self
This current
      And in this moment complete
Me
Takes her face
In hands controlled by only this current, complete me
And kisses her
All over
Eyebrows, freckles, her one dimple
Her lips
Warm and wet with coffee
I hate coffee

But it tastes good on her
Rich
Instead of bitter

They're always here
Usually quiet
Just a weight
Like a hand on my shoulder
Whispers I don't understand
They're here
Like the smell of smoke
Scary
Only when there's fire

There is no fire
Now
Right now
They are quiet
But never quite quiet enough
To be forgotten
I feel them
All of them
They surge around me
In a way I don't understand
Nothing at all but still too much

She doesn't know about them
I don't know how I would explain
If I could

If it was allowed
It sounds
It sounds
Like madness
I know it
And I know
She would believe it

There's a lot she doesn't know
About me
About us
She doesn't know about the blood
In or out
In my veins or in my fridge
She doesn't know about the sharpness
Of my tongue
Of my teeth

She knows only my softest parts
The parts that I want to show her
Want to give her
Want to place in her palms
And wrap her fingers around
The parts worth protecting
The parts worth sharing

But there are so many parts
So many pieces
She can't know about

And the urge to tell her
To show her
Is rare
But when it fights
It fights with a strength
I can't find
Anywhere else
In my weak little self

So I go away
I close up
Shut down
I get
Cold
And when I come back
Every time
I think
Maybe
She's already seen the real
Worst of me

Maybe it isn't the sharpness
The red on my lips
The glint of my teeth

And every time
I think
Be a little colder
Freeze a little harder
Push her away

Don't do it again
But the soft parts
The soft parts
They cling
They cry and ache and
Every time
I fall into her
And I whimper my apologies
Over and over
And she kisses my softness
And pulls the blankets over my sharpness
And thaws my coldness
And it begins again

I feel them
Today
Heavy
Pressing
On my shoulders
Hands on my chest
Lips to my ears
Blocking out everything but them
I'm sad
I'm sad in a way that makes my knees buckle
If I don't will them to stay
Keep me up
Hold me up
I'm sad

Today
And maybe it's their fault
I decide it is
The weight of them
Their terrible hunger
I'm sad
Today
Today
I can't ignore
That I'm not enough
For them
And that some day
I'll join them
And my hunger
Will wrap around a neck
My neck
 our neck
And squeeze

We keep one thing
Each of us
We pick it before we go
And start over
And we put it in a box
And we keep the boxes
Together
Always together
And if we ever

Felt ourselves slip
If we woke
A little outside ourselves
A little off
A little less
We'd open the box
And let our hands
Find what they needed
Let it soothe whichever part of us is shifting us around
Frantic and stuck and lonely and stuck
Show them
Something
One thing
At least
Remains
Of who they are
Of who they were
Let it soothe
Let it soothe
Let it soothe
Until we click back
Into place

I felt
Invincible
Before
When they were
A little further away

Before the sharpness in my mouth
Erupted
Broke through my gums
Snagged my lips
And made them bleed
I felt
Invincible

Kill me
I'd think
Kill me
I'd snarl at the tiniest threat
Kill me
It won't matter
I'll be
Right back
A shiny new me
No dust
No ash
No flame
No soil
Kill me
If you want,
You can't do it
In any way
That counts
For anything

I don't feel invincible
anymore

Mostly
I feel
Trapped
The soil won't welcome me
The fire won't take me
I'm not invincible
I'm not special
Not in the ways I boasted
I'm just
Here
In a body
In a life
And I don't know what to do with it
And they try to tell me
But they don't know either
And I'd hand it over
I think
Some days
I'd give it to one of them
Sink quietly into a corner
But I'm not invincible
And in there
Is much scarier
Than out here

She is for me
I tell them
As she nestles into my neck

She is for me
I tell them
This
Is for me
This
Is mine
I tell them
I tell them
Though it sounds
Like a question

Like asking permission
To have
Something
Someone
Of my own
And I wish I could smell her hair
And let no one else smell it
No one
Inside me or outside of me
And I wish I could kiss her
And feel only
What I feel
Not the heartbreak of lives forgotten by everyone
But a sad soul in my chest
I want
To just
Be
Be here
Be with her

Just me
Just me
And her
And no one else
And nothing else
And her hand finds my face
In the dark
And I thought she was asleep
But she's pulling me down
So my lips meet hers
And I try my hardest
To feel
Loud and hard and clear
To keep this feeling
In my hands
On my skin
In my mouth
Her tongue meeting mine
Her teeth biting my lips
I try to feel it and keep it
And feel it and
Keep it
All for me
All for me

Surely
Love should feel
Familiar to me

Surely
I must have felt it before
because I recognise the beginning
The first twist in my middle
The first quickening of my tired heart
The first urge to reach out
Holding my hand firm by my side
But feeling that pull
That pull
I know that pull
I've felt it before
Not with this hand
Not in this life
But I've felt it
A little part of my control
Slipping away
A little part of my composure
My shyness
Little bits
That I'm better off without
Because with them gone
    Or softened
    Muted
    At least
I can feel
My heart thud
Almost as hard
As it would
If it were like hers
And I wonder

If it feels like hers
In other ways too
If her heart
Feels like mine
Like mine does
Right now
The soft sense of urgency
The cautious excitement
The mix
The mess
The warmth
The warmth
The warmth
I hope she feels it too
That warmth

Surely
Love should feel
Familiar to me
Surely
I must have felt it before
Because I recognise the beginning
But the further we fall
The tighter we squeeze
The harder we hold
The more
Unfamiliar
It feels

A stranger in my veins
quick and sure
It's new
It's new
I know it
It's new
I have never loved like this
I have never loved
Like this

Five

There so much I want to tell her
It
Mostly
I want to tell her
It
The big truth
The big secret
I want her to know
And I want it to come from my lips
I want to whisper it
Only to her
Low and quiet and hot
I want to feel the goosebumps
On her skin
Hear her gasp a little
Feel her shiver
Feel her fear
Or her curiosity
Or her hatred
I want to feel
Whatever she feels
Whatever
She will give

But there's so much
More

So much
More
There's so much
I want her to know
I want her to know
How it feels
When the sharpness first breaks through your skin
How it feels
How I imagine
The first time they break
Through someone else's
The warmth
The comfort
The silence
The rhythm of it
How wrong it is
How right

I want her know what it tastes like
On my tongue
How smoothly it glides
Down my throat
How it weighs me down
Heavy in my stomach
Keeping me
Holding me
Settling me

How strong I am
When I'm whole

How much better
I can be
When I allow myself
To be worse
For those
Few moments

How much I want it
How much
I want it
How much I want
Her
Most of all
How much I want
To bite and suck and hold and
How much
How much
I hope
I never do

I haven't told her
I don't plan to
I just
Hold myself back
Just a little
Always
Hold my tongue
Hold back

and hope that
What's left of me
The bits I can share
Will be enough

Six

I don't mean to tell her
I promise
I don't
But I have always
Been more honest
In the dark
And in the dark
With her arms around me
And a blanket
Over our heads
I am honest
I am too honest
I am honest
And she listens
And I talk
And she listens
And I talk
And then she says

I knew there was something

And then

Thanks for telling me

And I choke on air
And I laugh

And she laughs
And she knows
She knows
And she shouldn't
She shouldn't she shouldn't
She shouldn't
But she does
She does
And I sense no fear
Hiding in the darkness
Feel no stiffness in the limbs thrown over me
She just knows
Now
And it feels
Scary
And it feels
Nice
To be known
It feels nice

She kisses my cheek
Runs a finger over my bottom lip
Sighs
Then begins
Question after question
I worry my answers aren't enough
That the idea is so much more
Interesting

Than the truth
That I am just
Here
With her
A little sharper
A little colder
No wiser
No smarter
No better
No no no
Just here
With her

But she seems
Pleased
Entranced
Impressed
And I think I like that
I think I
Do

The questions
Keep coming
And I answer them all
I'm telling her
I'm telling her

Everything
And Henry will know
I know
He will
And he won't be happy
I know he won't
But she will
She will

She asks about the sharpness
She asks to see
So I show
In the dim light from
The moon we let in on the secret
They glint
It glints
And her eyes do too
And she asks
          Can I touch
In a Voice
          In this Voice
And I try to say no
But I nod anyway
I nod and her hand comes up
And her finger
Nudges my lips
And they part
And her finger

Is in my mouth
And I'm panicking
And I'm not ok
And I

Bite

I bite

And she gasps

And I gasp

And she winces

And I fly from the bed and the light is on and I'm panicking
    I'm panicking
And there's this

Drop
Of
Blood
On
My
Tongue
And
I Can't
Bring myself
To swallow it
Not yet not now not at all

But I do
I do
Of course I do

And I feel it
Like an ember
In my throat
My chest
My stomach
I feel it
And I like it
And I want it
And I
I sit on the floor

I press my back to the wall
I don't know what I'm doing
I don't know
And when I look at her
She's staring at me
Her finger in her mouth
And I laugh
Because I'm jealous
And that feels
Funny
To me
In the
Moment
And her eyes widen
And then she
Laughs too
And we laugh
And we
Laugh

She drags me back to the bed
Says I'm a fool
But a cute one
Says it's fine
Says it's her fault
And I don't believe her
But I don't say so

I didn't mean to tell her
I didn't want her to know
I didn't
I didn't
And I'm not looking at her neck
I'm not
And I'm not thinking
Of the fizz
Of that one drop
In my stomach
In my chest
In my throat
On my tongue
I'm not thinking
About her skin
About vanilla
And rain
About the smell of her hair
About freckles
About breath
About blood
I'm not
I'm not
I'm not

Where does it usually come from
She asks
And I miss it
The first time

Because I'm preoccupied
Not thinking about her finger
About her wrists
About the map of veins on her forearm
And she asks again
And I blink
And tell her
I don't know
Henry takes care of it
Henry takes care of us
And she nods
And she wrinkles her brow
And she says

"So
You've never..."

I shake my head
I look at my feet
I look at the carpet
I look at my hands
I shake my head
"But
Don't you
Want
To?"
I shake my head

I look at my feet
I look at the carpet
I look at my hands
I nod my head
I nod
And I look up
And I expect fear
Repulsion
But she's
Looking at me
With sad eyes
She's looking at me
With what I can only recognise
As pity
And I don't know how to respond

I do want it
Of course I want it
Everything in me
Whines for it
Craves and cries
But I know the rules
I know why we have the rules
I know why I can't
Shouldn't
Won't
Wouldn't
I know

I know
But I want
I want to feel
What I'm supposed to feel
Built to feel
I want to feel strong and still and quiet
I want to feel fierce and full
I want to take
Be given
Take
I want it
I want it
But I can't
Shouldn't
Won't

And I tell her so

"But it's ok
To need
What you need"
She says
As though I need
A cookie
A cheat day
A nap
And I laugh
Then regret it

I say sorry
I say
It's different
I say
If I can take
Without causing hurt
Without taking
More than I should
More than I need
Then that's what I should do
That's all I can do
Will do
Want to do
But she doesn't look convinced
Of course she doesn't
Because she always knows
When I'm lying

"What if"
She says
In a new voice
"Someone wants
To give"

I look at the floor
I shake my head

I shake my head
I shake my head
I try to ignore her
As politely as I can
I try to ignore her
And the images
Flashing in my head
Sharpness
Wetness
Fullness
Quiet
Power
Quiet

I shake my head
She takes my hand
Her fingers
Take my chin
Move my head so we're face to face
She kisses me
I try to shake my head
She kisses me
I try
She kisses me
I kiss her
Her fingers on my chin
Her hand holding mine
Her tongue

Her tongue in my mouth
Slowly
Slowly
Licking over my teeth
The sharpness
The sharpness
I kiss her
I kiss her
I kiss her

what do you do with love like this
what do I do with love like this
how do I hold it
how do I keep it
how do I stop it

I suck
I pull
I drag
I suckle
She pets my head
She brushes my hair from my face
I suck
I pull
I drag
I suckle

She whispers
And winces
And I suck and she
Says
Don't stop
And she says
It's ok
And I suck and I pull and I drag and I
Suckle
I am not here
I am real and unreal
I am quiet and loud and I am
Floating
I am floating and
I am here I am
Here I am
Here

I stop when her hand stops
Petting my head
I stop when her whimpering fades away
I stop
But I stay where I am
I lap over the marks I've made
I try to make them heal
Make them close
I know
I know it doesn't work like that

But I try
I try
I try to make it not hurt
Anymore
I try
I promise
I try

I whisper into her neck
I whisper to myself
Never again
Not again
No more
No more
No more
I tell myself
I tell her
I ask myself
I beg
Never again
I promise
I try
I promise

I don't feel real
I feel hot

Under my skin
I feel wild and
Tamed and kept and held and
Free and
I feel
So much
Everything stands
Too still
Everything moves
Too fast
I feel good and
I feel good
I don't know
That I'm real
But I don't know
That I'm not

She wakes with me wrapped around her
She wakes with my hands on her cheeks
My eyes locked on hers
Our feet are tangled
I'm breathing so fast
She's breathing so slowly
She asks
If I'm ok
And I nod
I nod
Because I am

I am
Ok
I am real and here and ok
And she is real and here and ok
And I kiss her I kiss
Her I kiss
her

what do you do with love like this
what do I do with love like this
how do I hold it
how do I keep it
how do I stop it

Seven

It's a need
Now
After
It's a need
I feel the tips of my teeth
Scrape them over my tongue
Again and again
Focusing on the scrape
The burn
It had to be thirst
It had to be hunger
It stirred in my stomach
It made my head spin
But it wasn't
Unpleasant
If anything
It felt
Nice
Warm
It roared
But didn't snarl
I look at her
At her neck
At her wrist
The crook of her elbow
But my eyes

Don't
Can't
Linger
This wasn't what they wanted
I look up
I look at her lips
I look at the way her bottom lip
Glistens
At the redness
Where her teeth held firm
I drag my eyes to meet hers
To find them
Focused on me
On my lips
Oh
Oh it is hunger
My body heaves with the realisation
Relief at my finally catching up
Finally recognising its signals
Oh it is need and want and need and
Want

Eight

The museum was Henry's idea
Not the statues
Just the museum
Henry likes quiet places
Libraries
Museums
The park in the early morning
The kitchen before Freddie wakes up

The first time he brought me here
I was sulking
I was young
Younger
Newer
Louder
I thought I was sharp
But I was blunt
I was baby teeth
I was heavy and soft
A bruise of a person
I was sulking
I was tired of the rules that kept me safe
I was tired of being seen
All the time
Watched
I wanted to be sharp and fast and alone

I did not
Want to be in the museum
So I huffed
And I called every painting stupid
Every sculpture ugly
And I called Henry both
And Henry ignored me
And stared at every painting
Like they were the gravestone
Of someone he'd once loved
And when I returned
For the first time
Years later
I wondered
If maybe they were

The first time I came here by myself
Was early on a Tuesday
I'd been allowed to leave alone
For a few months
By then
And already
I was bored
Already
I thought
I'd exhausted the city
Been everywhere
Seen everything

A couple months of freedom
And I thought
I knew this city
Better than anyone else
I was wrong
But I was young
So it didn't matter

I don't know why
I went to the museum
My feet just
Brought me there
And then the following week
They did it again
And a few days later
They did it again
And after the visit
When I realised
I knew each painting by name
I had to admit
I brought myself there
That really
I liked it
That really
I found comfort in the paintings
Friends in the sculptures
That I found peace
In the echo of my footsteps
On the marble floor

My favourite sculpture
At first
Was a woman
Tall and strong
Holding her hand out
Towards me
Her eyes
I thought
Should look empty
Should be empty
But I felt seen by her
I felt
That she could see all of me
That I could stand in front of her
And be seen
So seen
That I could
Give myself away
For a minute
I could let myself be
Whatever this woman saw in me
So I stood
And I let myself be seen
By grey stone eyes
Old and cold and beautiful
Then I left
And I forgot all about her
Until the next week
When I visited her again
And gave her more of me

To see
To take
To keep
To have

When I've given her all I can
I move on
To the next one
A man
Holding a shield
His face contorted with pain
I give him even more
I give him so much
His face seems to change
Though I know
It doesn't
Hasn't
Won't

I find more
Learn more
And I give to them all
I give it all
All the memories
The half dreams
Habits and talents and selves

I take them from myself
And I give them all
To these
solid people
Sealed lips and cold hands
Smooth and strong and better
Than I am
Than I
Could be

And I tell these pieces
As I hand them over
This will be better
For you
They will be better for you
Someone empty
But not hollow

They never stay
But I decide
In myself
That they have
They did
These sad selves inside me
Living new lives
In beautiful bodies
Sculpted by talented hands
Finally being seen once again

I ignore them when they cry
They are not here
I tell myself
You are not here
I tell them
You are somewhere
New
Somewhere old and
Somewhere better

I give and I give and I give
But I don't empty
So I give and I give
Until I can pretend
There is quiet
Somewhere
Inside me

Nine

I sink in
I sink into her
Sharpness
Softness
Full and whole and
I sink in
And I take
And I take and I
Take
Until I'm closer to full
Until she's closer to empty
And I think maybe
That means
We're closer to being
The same

My eyes are brighter
Her eyes sunken
Just a little

And when I finish
When I lick my lips clean
And take a deep breath
And look at her

And I love her
More than I've ever loved anyone
And I know
It's the warmth
Racing through my cold veins
And the waking of my tired heart
But I don't care
I decide it's her
It's her
All her
And I look into her tired eyes
And I tell her so
And I wonder
For a single second
If that's right
If that's fair
If I'll live to regret it
But I do it
I lisp around my sharpness
And I tell her and I
Tell her
And she smiles
And whispers it back
Her voice
Deeper
Raspy
Drained
Drained
Drained
Then she smiles

And collapses in my lap
Soft breaths on the back of my knee
Hair spread out on my thighs
Her weight
Her skin
I trace a vein on her forearm
I trace a vein on mine
I lift her hand to my mouth
I kiss her fingertips
A giggle
Manic and sharp
Escapes me
Bursts from me
I try to catch it
Slap a hand to my mouth
I smile behind my palm
Everything is quiet
I close my eyes
Hear her breathe
Hear the blood pumping around me
Everything is quiet
It's just us
It's just me

When Claudia wakes
I make her French toast
And we sit in the kitchen
And ignore Freddie

Singing as he stirs
Flour in the air like warm breath in the cold
Milk on the floor
Sugar in his hair
He sings
Claudia eats
I sit
And buzz
I buzz
My bones shake
My blood
Moves
So fast
I'm all
Movement
I'm going and going and going
But I sit
And I ignore Freddie
And I watch Claudia eat
And I'm going I'm going
I'm going

I come back
When she's asleep
They come back
When the house is quiet
And the stars are out
And the duvet is too heavy on my limbs

And my limbs are too heavy
And I am too heavy
And I am too still
Too still
My bones
My bones
Weigh me down
And they're coming back
And they're waking
And they're talking to me
Whispering
And they're hungry
And they want
They want
They want so badly
And I want
I want to give them what they need
What they need
To be sated
To be quiet
To be
Quiet

She moans
Crinkles her brow
Licks her lips
Turns around
Buries her face in her pillow

And is silent again
And I watch her hair
Slip off her neck
And I look
At the two
Tiny marks
tiny
So tiny
So small
I'm staring
And I can't stop
And they're staring back
And my bones
Are so heavy
And my head
Is so full
And they are so
Small
And my heart
Is so
slow
And my blood
Is sludge beneath my skin
Lava
Sleet
I don't know
I don't know
Smoke
Maybe
Just smoke

And they are so
Small
And my hand is reaching out
And my breathing
Is heavy
And my fingers
are cold on her skin
And I'm shaking her
Gentle
Quietly frantic
And I whisper
Please hold me?
And she smiles
And turns
Hides the two little marks
In the pillow I now call hers
And wraps herself around me
And I can breathe
And I can focus
On her skin
Instead of mine
The weight of her
The weight of her
And I close my eyes
And I listen to her breathe
And I sleep

Freddie and Claudia
Insist on hugging
For at least a minute
Standing at the front door
Freddie
Listing all the recipes he's
Mastered
And asking her to please
Rank them
So he knows
Exactly what to make
Next time she visits
And the time after
And the time –
And I poke him in the ribs
Until he unleashes her
And he sighs
And says
Text me your favourites
And pats her on the head
And returns to the kitchen

I kiss her goodbye
And I say thank you
And I kiss her goodbye
And I say thank you
And I kiss her
And I say thank you

And she kisses me goodbye
And says to stop thanking her
And she kisses my neck
Just below my ear
And looks me in the eyes
And leaves
And I stand
And I try to breathe
And I try to tell myself
That what I'm feeling
Is love
Love love love
For her
For her
For her
For Claudia
For her
That what I'm feeling
Is love
Not hunger
Not a craving
That I'm missing her
Already
And not the spread of blood
Over my tongue
That my heart
Is rioting
Old and slow and weary
But fighting
In my chest

Saying follow follow follow
Saying go
We miss her
Her
Her
Her
Not the red on my lips
Not the thickness
Sliding down my throat
Not the quiet
The quiet
The quiet
The quiet

I'm certain Henry knows
I knew he would
He always does

So I avoid him

Ten

Freddie
Has been Freddie
For twenty-three years
Already
And Freddie
Is soft
And Freddie
Is sad
Kind and angry
Sweet and lonely
Freddie is the best
The worst
And Freddie
Is mine
My Freddie
My friend
My brother
My Freddie
And I wish
He could remember that
All of the time
But he can't

Freddie forgets
And when Freddie forgets

Freddie
Leaves
And when he remembers
Freddie comes home
Bruised and full
Belly full of blood
Heart full of regret
And those are things
Freddie can't forget

When Freddie goes
He goes broken

When Freddie's returns
He returns
Patched together
Glue and tape and determination

He cries and he moans and he sits
On the bathroom floor
And we bandage up the bits he missed
And with all our hands
We hold him together
Until it sticks

And I wonder
If I leave broken
Could I
Will I

Would I
Return fixed
Will I return
New or old
Or better or worse
Or
Will I return
At all
If I leave

But Freddie
Hasn't left
In a while
And part of me says
This is progress
The part that trusts
What he says
This is progress
This is growth
This is good
The sweet part says
The hopeful part
The part that has a talent
For blocking out the rest

The rest
The rest
Says this

Is overdue
Says this isn't good
This stretch
This extra time
This
Just means
Next time
It'll be worse
It'll be longer
Harder
Bloodier
Scarier
The rest
Says prepare
Says be careful
Says hug him tighter
Love him harder
Don't let go
Don't
Let go

I compliment his food a little more
Make extra mmms
And ahhs
Eat a little more
Do everything
But lick the plate clean
And he just looks at me

Like he knows
Exactly what I'm doing
And why I'm doing it
So he scowls a bit
Rolls his eyes a bit
Then looks back down
At his still full plate
Takes just a sip of blood

                Not enough
                Not enough

Mutters a soft
Sorry
And leaves

And Henry and I look at each other
And I know
He doesn't want me to mention it
It's in the stiffness of his back
The set of his shoulders
The crease between his eyebrows
So I keep quiet
And wait for him to leave first
Because the idea of getting up
And leaving him alone
Doesn't sit right
In my too full stomach
So I wait
Until he pushes his chair back
Considers saying
Something

Hums instead
And leaves

And what do I do
What do I do
What have I ever done
Have I ever done
Anything

I want to chase after them
Which one I don't know
I want to ask
Tell
Beg
Please
Which one
I don't know

All I know
Is I want them
Here
Here and safe and
Here
With me
With us

And what do I do
What do I do

What have I ever done
Have I ever done
Anything

I go to my room
I sit on my bed
I wonder if tonight is a night for sleep
I hope it is
I ask it to be
But it doesn't respond

I stand outside his room
I think of what to say
I roll words around on my tongue
I say them
Very quietly
Only to the air
The wood of the door
I wish they would
Slip through the keyhole
Slide under the door
But I say them
Too quietly
And I know
They never stood a chance

And in the morning
When Freddie's door is open
And his bed is made
And the kitchen is cold
And his key is gone
I try to tell myself
Convince myself
They never stood a chance
Those words
In the air
In the wood
In my mouth
They never stood a chance
We never stood a chance
I never stood a chance

Henry makes breakfast
He sighs a lot
He tells me not to play with my food
Like I'm a child
And a part of me
Is angry
And a part of me
Is relieved

Eleven

I miss Freddie
I worry
I feel
Like I'm missing

I sleep in his bed
Even though I don't need sleep
Yet
And I lie
And I doze
And I
I miss him and I
Miss him and I
Miss him

Henry doesn't mention him
Never does
But he's stiff
He looks down more
He doesn't hum as much

He does it differently
But he misses him and
He misses him and
He misses him

I don't mention him much
I did the last time
And it made it worse
So I don't
Mention him
Much

We just miss him
Together

Claudia
Doesn't understand
Really
And I can't explain
Really
But she hugs me
Extra
And she kisses me
Slower
And I hold her
Harder

Closer
Until I imagine
We merge
Until I imagine
We are something
Different
Together
Something quiet and good and sweet and kind and we
sleep and we eat and we smile and we sleep and we eat
and we smile and we sleep and we eat and we smile
and we sleep and we eat and we smile and
That's it
That's all
We just are
This thing
We just are
And it's easy
It's easier

After the first week
I decided it's time
It's time to come home
That was long enough
Now Freddie
I tell him
I tell him
It's time
To come home

But he doesn't listen
He doesn't listen and he doesn't come home
And Henry doesn't mention him
And Claudia kisses me slower
And slower and slower until
Time seems to stop
Time seems to
Stop
And I hold her
Closer
Closer
Harder
Harder
Until maybe we merge
Maybe we merge
Or maybe we go right
Through
Each other
Until we're standing
Back to back
Until we aren't
Looking at each other
At all
Anymore
And the rose has withered
And we kiss
So slowly
And Henry is so quiet and I am so
Tired and Claudia
Doesn't understand

Really
And I don't hold it
Against her
really

I am bad
I think
I am bad

Twelve

I'm crying
And I hate it
And I hate myself for it
And she's holding my face
Hands on my cheeks
Thumbs trying to catch the tears
And I hate it
And I hate myself for it
For the need
The want
For the fact that the want
Outweighs the need
For the fact that they both
Outweigh the guilt
And her hands
On my cheeks
Are hot
And they smell like
They smell like
Vanilla
Or honey
Or
Blood
Blood
They smell like blood
And they don't

And I know that
But the need
And the want
Say
Blood
Vanilla
Honey
Blood
They say
Vanilla
Honey
Blood
Bite
Bite
Take

I don't take
I won't take
I want
I need
I won't

I want
I need
I don't

I don't

I do.

Her hands are in my hair
And she pulls
And she whimpers
And I whimper
And it's ok
It's ok
She's ok
And I'm ok
I'm ok
I'm taking what I need
Only what I need
I tell my sharpest parts
Only what I need
Only what you need
Only what we need
No more
No more
Please no more
And it's so much
What we need
It's so much
Filling my mouth

Filling me
Filling me
Then her hand falls
From my hair
And her whimpers sound
Different
Weaker
And I stop
And I stop
I stop
I stop
Finally
I stop

I wrench myself away
I wipe my mouth clean
I lick the blood from my hands
Turned away from her
Shame hot in my chest
Desire hotter
I lick myself clean
And maybe later it'll hit me
The potency of this moment
How far I've gone
How I cannot seem to have
Without taking
Maybe

Claudia is mumbling
And I can hear her
I can
But
In this moment
I know
The want
Is bigger than the need
And I won't
I won't take
Only for want
I won't
So I block out her mumbling
Sticky hands over my ears
Like a toddler
The pathetic temptation to sing
La la la
To cover her weak little voice
So strong I have to bite my tongue
To stop myself

When I turn
Finally
She's half asleep
Still mumbling
Murmuring
Maybe
I can't tell what she's saying

If she's saying anything
But she's frowning
Just a little
And she has tears
Drying on her cheeks
And my stomach lurches
And so much of me
Wants to give it all up
Give it all back
Be empty
But so much of me
Refuses to let go
And I swallow hard
And I swallow harder
And I keep it all in
Then I sweep her into my arms
And I wrap myself around her
And I breathe in time with her
And I whisper apologies into her hair
And try
To ignore the buzzing
Under my skin
And the lightness of my bones
And how much
Better I feel

Thirteen

He comes back
Late at night
He falls into his bed
Beside me
And we look at each other
In the dark
And I don't see the bruises or the blood
Or the sharpness or the sharpness or
The sharpness
I see Freddie
I see my
Freddie
And we sleep

We wake early
And we look at each other
And still
I don't see the bruises or the blood or the sharpness
We look at each other
And we sleep

We wake late
And we look at each other
And I see the bruises and the blood and the
Sharpness
And I cry
A little
And he cries
A little
And we lie
And we cry
And we lie
And we cry
And then we get up
And he bathes
And I make him coffee
And Henry asks how he is
And I don't ask how he knows
And I just
Shrug
And he just
Hums
And we nod
And we drink blood
Warm and heavy
From our biggest mugs
Chug the last of it
When we hear footsteps
On the stairs

When Freddie comes downstairs
He's stolen one of my T-shirts
The fabric tight around his arms
He rubs the hem between his finger and thumb
His socks belong to Henry
He won't look at us

We look at him like we're scared he'll
Vanish
Like the desperate sadness we felt
Became its own person
Like it twisted itself into
What we need most
Want most
Miss most
We look at him
Like we're scared
He looks at the floor
Like he is too

It takes three winces
Too hot coffee
Toast on a split lip
A clumsy elbow meeting a sturdy table
Three winces
And Henry breaks

He's up like the wind has taken him
And he has Freddie's face in his hands
His fingers move over every graze
Bruise scab slice
Nose chin cheek
Then that face is buried in Henry's
Chest
Cry sob scream
And I leave

I buy Freddie a rose
Red
And I buy
Flour
And eggs
And butter
Chocolate
Just in case
I walk around
I walk and I
Walk
And I find myself outside the flower shop
And I feel Claudia's hands on me
Hear her say
She's so happy he's back
Feel her lips on my
Eyes cheek chin
I don't go in

I take what I need
What I can get
From knowing
She's there
Having a day
Having a life
And I bring no badness
Into it
Today
I just walk

I make a cake with Freddie
He's weak
And he sits most of the time
And we don't
Talk
But we
talk
And we even laugh
Now and then
And I don't ask
And he doesn't tell
We just make
A lumpy cake
With grainy icing
And we write
Welco
Because we made the icing letters too big

And we laugh
And he gets food colouring on my shirt
And he splits his lip when a giggle erupts
And he bangs his stupid elbow again
And he's tired
And he's tired
And I'm too awake
And he is here
He is here
With me
With us
And we laugh
And we eat
The whole cake
All but one slice
Which we know Henry won't eat
But will appreciate
And he's here and he's here and he's
Here

Fourteen

They fell in love once
When lives aligned

Just once

They love
Always
But they fell in love
Just once
They lived a life with their arms around each other
They lived that life
Like they'd been waiting for it
Willing it
To come to them

They lived that life like something
Right in the centre of them
Knew it would happen
And knew
It wouldn't happen again

They asked me
One night
Near the end

When they felt it
Start to burn beneath their skin
When they felt it
Mercifully
At the same time
After the years they had watched over me
And filled me up with all the goodness
This one good, good life had given them
They asked me
With tenderness they usually reserved
Only for each other
To please
Remember
But never to remind
To try my best
Try my hardest
To remember
How they loved
How they held each other's fingers
How they held each other's gaze
How they chose each other
Over and over
Prioritised each other
Cared for each other
How they grew together
Lived together

I don't know
How clearly I remember
How many details I've forgotten

But no matter how many lives I live
I won't forget
Not fully
Not ever
And I won't tell them

Sometimes
It's best to forget
The good things
Too

We know we hold secrets
For each other
We know
We hold whole histories
For each other
Identities and memories
relationships and losses and mistakes and
victories and versions
Shame and pride and lightness and the deepest darknesses
We lose and we lose and we lose
And we try and we try and
We try
To hold on
To what we can
We don't judge each other
We have no right to
We know too much

We've seen too much
We've done too much
We just try
We just try
To remember
We just try
To hold pieces of each other
Safe inside ourselves
So after life
After life
After life
Our togetherness
Is what makes us three
Incomplete people
As close to complete as we
Could ever be

Fifteen

Claudia
Is loud
I hadn't ever noticed
Really
Until today
Until the museum
Until her voice fills
The big empty room
And I imagine all the sculptures
All the stone people
Turning to look at us
And I blush

Claudia is loud
She loves this painting
So she tells it so
This one confuses her
So she asks it questions
This one moves her
So she cries
This one amuses her
So she laughs
She is loud and full and too
Alive
I think
Too alive to be here

And suddenly
I want her out
I don't want her here
Among us
Us old and heavy people
And I regret ever
Suggesting she come with me
Ever so much as mentioning the museum
I regret and I seethe

Claudia
Is too loud
Too alive
Too honest and pure in everything she is and feels and
    says and does
And I am jealous and I want her
Out

But her face
Her eyes
Put the stone ones to shame
The ones I feel so seen by
Have nothing on hers
They're bright and alive and when they look at me
When she looks at me
I don't feel seen
I feel known

So when she looks at me
She knows
She knows my thoughts have soured
My feelings bubbled over
And she sighs
And takes my hand
And I feel
I know
I am terrible
I am terrible
For ever wanting a moment
Without her

We stay for hours
Her favourites are paintings
I've never really looked at
Sculptures I've wandered past
Acquaintances
Not friends
But she looks at them
Like they're family
And I tell them
It's a pleasure to meet them
Properly
And that I'll be sure to visit again

I introduce her to my collection
To the strong woman in the flowing dress
The pained man with his shield

I don't tell her what they are
What they are to me
But I tell her
They are important
They are special
And I wonder if that's true
If the selves I've handed over
Are important
Are special
If they matter to me
I thought they didn't
But as I point them out
And as I watch her take in every inch of their smooth
    stone skin
I think that really
They must
And that's new
And that's strange
And that's nice
Nicer
And I hope
The feeling stays
And I hope she stays
The more she sees
The more she learns
The more I show
Tell
Share
I hope
She stays

Sixteen

Why does he leave
Where does he go
She asks
And I shrug
And she asks again
And I shrug
And I say
Because he's brave
And stupid
And weak
Sometimes
Sometimes he is weak and brave
And they're
Dangerous
Together
Dangerous
Together

I don't know where he goes
I just know
He goes
And I worry
And he comes back
And I worry

Don't you want to
She asks
Don't you want to
Go
And I shrug
And she asks again
And I shrug
And I say
I can't
And she says
That doesn't answer the question
And I shrug
And I nod

Let's go
She says
Let's go
Like it's an option
Like its real
Like something exists outside the city
Outside the rules
Like something exists for me
Like I could exist
Somewhere else
Like we could

She says
Let's go
She says
I'll show you
I'll show you
So much
She says
Let's go
And I shrug
And I nod
And I go

We go

We take her aunt's car
Then a train
Then we walk
And we walk
And I try
Not to think about
Henry
About Freddie
I try to tell myself
It's ok
I'm ok
We're ok
They're ok

I try to tell myself
It doesn't scare me
Being away from them
Being
Without them
I try

We walk
And we walk
And then

We are in a forest
I tell her
As if
Somehow
She isn't aware

She laughs
Soft and light
It bounces off trees
Bounces around us
And she takes my fingers
In her hand
Our hands
To her lips

She kisses each of my
Knuckles
Then puts my hand
On the trunk of a tree
The biggest tree
I've ever seen
Ever
Ever
I know it
I feel it
So I feel the tree
I close my eyes
Feel how strong it is
How firm and tough
But blanketed
In moss
Soft and dense

We are in a forest
I tell myself
As if
Somehow
I'm not aware
Yes
We are
She says
And I laugh

And I laugh
And I keep my hand on the tree

And with my other hand
I pull her closer
Wrap an arm around her waist
Pull her close
Smell her vanilla
And the forest
Vanilla
And the forest
And I feel
So much
And I feel
So much
And I feel
So good
And I feel
Myself
And only myself

And for once
For once
For the very
Very first time
They are silent
It is silent
Because for the first time
The very first time
They have nothing to say

They
Have not been here
They have nothing left
here

Here is
Mine
Here is Claudia's
Here is Ours
ours ours
Only ours
And it is quiet
And it is quiet
And it is quiet

Everything is
New
Everything is
Fresh
It smells different
It feels different
It feels good
It feels
It feels like Claudia feels
It feels real
It feels alive

It feels
Alive
And I want
I want to
Stay
I want to stay
I tell each tree
Each leaf
Please please let me stay

Claudia takes me to a cabin
It's cold
And then so warm
Strange
And then home
So quickly
So suddenly

She lights the fire
And I boil the kettle
She takes food from her bag
Soup and bread and cheese and
I pile blankets in front of the fire
And we forget the food
For a while
We don't feel our hungry stomachs

We feel wool and skin and breath and hands
We feel each other
Ourselves
We feel
Good
And
Warm
And whole

We eat bread and cheese for dinner
Because we are lazy
And full in so many ways
That this one type of hunger
Hardly seems to matter

We sleep in front of the fire
And wake to ash in the hearth
Our breath before our faces
We light the fire again
Fall asleep again
Hold each other again
We wake again
To flame and heat
Our breath wet on each other's necks
We eat we sleep we hold each other
We eat we sleep we take our fill

We take our fill
And when we are full
Of warmth of food of heat of us
We walk into the forest again

Seventeen

There is a statue
In the forest
Near the cabin
She stands beside a pond
Tall and beautiful
Cracks cover her arms
Dip into her stomach
Run down her legs
She is dust and moss and dirt
She is old
She is real
She is in this world
This world that lives and breathes and grows and changes
And here she can change too
Here
She can be worn down
She can be touched
Vines can grip her
Wind can shake her
She is not like the others
In the museum
Strong and quiet and perfect
Restored
Reserved
She changes
She changes

And if I tried to give myself to her
She would not take it
It would not stick
So I don't give
I take
I take her into me
Her wildness
Her realness
Her cracks and crumbles
She is me
Not the others
She is me
We are each other
We are broken and still standing
We are messy
We are here

Eighteen

By the third night
I've slept too much
Much too much
I'm restless
Jumpy
I need
I need
I don't know what I need
But I know
It is too quiet
It is too peaceful
I am restless
I am jumpy
I am
Here
In a forest
And I realise
For the first time
I don't know where I am
I don't know anything but
I am in a forest
And the forest has welcomed me
The cabin allowed me to call it home
But now
My ungrateful bones
Miss home

Miss walking through a city
Late at night
And seeing concern on strangers' faces
At such a young woman
Roaming the streets
So late
So so late
I miss the feeling of stealth
Of knowing I am more dangerous
Than anything they feared on my behalf
I miss
Freddie
I miss
Henry
I miss
Being me
Where I am me

The forest
The trees
This
All of this
This is Claudia
And it has taken me
Taken me in
Just like she did
It has wrapped itself around me
It has tried to hush the voices in my head
With its rustling
With its growing and moving and

It has taken me
In
It has taken me
In
And despite it
Despite the quiet
Despite the peace
I miss my home
I miss my noise
I miss my life

Henry
Fills the fridge
And we ask no questions
Someone
Older than Henry
Tells him
How to fill the fridge
And we ask no questions

We aren't alone
We just pretend
We aren't the most dangerous
We just
Pretend

When we feel weak
And restrained

When we feel
Bound and kept
When we feel like
Birds in cages
Dogs in muzzles
We pretend
We are softer than we are
We pretend we are harder
Than we are
But we know
We know the truth
So we stay together
We stay together
And together
We don't pretend
Together
We just are

It's always been
The way it is now
The house
The three
The home
The family
It has always been us
In all our forms
We raise each other
We move apart

We move together
We move apart
We come back
We come back
We hurt and we long and
We moan like we could survive
Any other way
We are
What we are
We pretend sometimes
Walking down the street
We smile at people
Like we are
The same
As them
Like we
Ever could
Be
We pretend
At the bookshop
Like so many of the spines
Don't boast names
That aren't ours anymore
We pretend
We pretend
But we come home
And we are known
Freddie leaves
But he comes back
Henry scolds

But he loves
I moan
But I am
This
I am this
I pretend
I pretend
In flower shops and museums and forests
I pretend
But I am this
I am
And I miss home
And I miss family
And I want to be
Just this

I let myself be taken
For another day
I let her arms hold me
I let the forest
Cover me
Hands in the earth
Heart in her hands
I let myself
Be taken
I let myself be kept
Soft and warm and held

I like pushing my hands
Down
Down
Into the dirt
Into the ground
Past the cold that rests on top
Down to the warmth
Down where the worms live
I like the worms
I like the insects
They crawl over my fingers and
I worry I've scared them
That I'm too big and too strong and too here
But I just hope I haven't
And I stay still
And let them move
Finger to finger
Tiny and alive and tickling

I like the trees
I love the trees
The trees are my favourite
To them
I am small
To them
I am weak
To them
I am small and weak but still
I am here

I rest my palms on their trunks
I push
And feel only my own muscles move
I push
And I feel small and weak and real
I feel
Like a person
Small
Weak
Human

I love the trees

There is a river
Barely a river really
A stream
Really
It trickles
In places
Over rocks
Around trees
Over my feet
Around my ankles

I stand in the stream
Until I can barely feel my toes
Until goosebumps run up my legs
I am cold and wet and real real real

I am cold
And wet
And real

In the cabin
We have a bath
We heat the water
Slowly
And fill the tub
Slowly
And we sink in
Slow and shy and pink cheeked
Pink from heat
Pink from
Pink from

We sink in
Together
I pull the ribbon from her hair
I free her hair from its plait
I run my fingers through it
Long and silky
Velvet in my hands
I lather
I massage
I rinse
I lather
I massage

I rinse
She leans against me
I put my arms around her
I feel her heartbeat as if it is my own
I feel her
As if she is mine
As if I am hers
As if
I feel as if
We are each other
Are each other's

We stay in the bath until it gets cool
We wrap ourselves in big scratchy towels
We rub our arms
Up down hard fast
We shiver in front of the fire
We tell jokes
So our laughter
Warms us
Inside out
We warm each other
We warm each other
We leave our towels by the fire
We trade them for sheets
We warm each other

We warm each other

Nineteen

But
I snap
But
I snap
But
I snap and
Maybe it's the quiet
Maybe it's the voices
And how sometimes
Maybe
I miss them
Maybe it's that
I take
Have taken
And she is pale
She is pale
Maybe it's the wind in the trees
Or the rain on the roof
I snap
I snap
I snarl
I bite
My words bite
She says
I love you
She says

Take
Take and
Take more
And I
Snap
She says I love you
And I snap
And I say

It's not me
Though

I wish hadn't shouted it
I wish I could stop the next words
Because I know
I'll shout those too

It's not me
All the things you like
All the things I know and do and think and feel
It's all just
Leftovers

She looks at me
Like she knows I'm right
And I feel
Defiant and smug and bruised
And then she softens
Her jaw unclenches
And she looks at me

Like she knows I'm right
And like she thinks
It just
Doesn't really
Matter

And I want to agree
I want to see it all
As just
One big life
Or as just
One little life
I want to see it all as mine
I want and I want
In a greedy, belligerent, childish way
I want to claim it all
I want to be it all
But I am
This
I am weak and insignificant and I have been
So much
And I have done so much
But really
Really
I have done nothing
Been nothing
And with every day
Here
In this body
In this

Self
I continue
To be
Absolutely nothing
Of value of worth of merit of

If you step back
If you walk away
And turn
And look
You will see
All of me
All the things and thoughts and lives and achievements and
All of it
And it will be
Staggering
And it will be
Impressive
But it will not
Be me

Because when you come closer
When you zoom in
When you
Really look
All you will see
Is me
This me
With my blurry memories and half-formed thoughts
With only hints of the talent and knowledge I should have

I have ruled and led and fought and won
I have innovated and inspired and influenced
I have been the best and the worst
Done the best and the worst
Seen the best and the worst
Felt the best and the worst

But come close
And come closer
And look
And you will see
None of it

I am wasted potential
I tell her
I could be more
I should be better
I could be
I should be
But I'm not
I'm not
I just take
I just take
And I
Am this
And this
Is all I am

Then I sit
And I cry
And I cry
And I tell her
I don't want to take
I tell her
I am taking
Too much
I tell her
I need to be
Different
I tell her
I need more
She needs more
I tell her
I tell her
I tell us

And I sit
And I cry
And I thank her
And I thank her
And she nods
And she holds me
And she lets me hold her
And we kiss
And I let myself feel it
The want and the need and the kiss and the kiss and
    the kiss

And we lie
And we kiss
And we hold each other
And we hold ourselves

I don't know
Who I am
I tell her
I don't know
And she says
That's ok
And she says
Sometimes
She doesn't either
And I decide
To let that help
I decide
To let her help
This
Us

Hold me please
Hold me
Please please
Hold me
I whimper
Small and soft and pathetic

Please
And she does
And she scoops me up and she
Takes me in
And I vanish into her
And I think about
All she is
How strong how kind how patient
And I think about how
I'm not ready for her
And how
I want to be
So I nestle in
And I say
I am not anything
Yet
I am new every day
And I am old every night
And I want to be yours
But I don't know how
And I blame and I rage and I hold
Too tight
And I'm sorry and can we
Can we try again

And I cross my fingers
And I listen to her breathe
And I wait and I want and I hold my own breath

And I hold her hand and I stroke her hair
And I hold and I wait and I hold and
She nods
And she says
I like you
Please see that
Please pay attention
To just how much
I like you
Not just how much
I love you

And we link our pinkies
And we kiss our knuckles
And we whisper
One more time
And we kiss and we kiss
And we kiss

Not yet
She says
And I feel the words
Warm on my neck
Sink into my pores
No thinking
Not yet

Just
Just
Stay with me for another minute
And I nod
And I wish
In a nasty
Sickening way
That she sounded sadder
Instead of comfortably resigned
Because that
Just seems so much worse

In the morning
I leave

Twenty

I say goodbye
To the trees
The dirt
The stream
I say goodbye
To the worms
To goosebumps and bathwater
And warmth warmth warmth

The walk to the train
Is just long enough
For guilt to kick in
For regret to sneak up
Behind me
A hand on my shoulder
My feet get heavier
But I walk

But I walk

I miss the dirt
When my feet hit concrete

I miss the stream when thirst
Pinches my lips
I miss the trees
I miss the trees
When the sky is too clear
When the sun beats
Too hard on my head
When heat pours down over me
When sweat collects
In the dip of collarbones
The small of my back

I miss the trees

The train ride back
Is loud
Some of them know trains
Some of them have memories
Kisses on trains
Dramatic goodbyes
The start of a new life
The end of a romance
So they come back
First
Wailing
They wail
They wail
So loud

Knowing they have me all to themselves
For now
Knowing
I will listen now
I will listen
Knowing I know what it is like now
To have something all your own
And to let that something go

I sit alone
And I let them scream
Let them moan and whine and whimper
Let them get
So loud
It hurts
Let it hurt
Let the noise
Pound against my skull
Let it drown out everything else I feel
Let it take over
Until I'm home
Until I'm safe
Until the regret loosens its grip

I read a book on the train
Poems

I found it
In the cabin
I read it
Every night I didn't sleep
Tucked in next to Claudia
Wide awake
Every morning before she woke
Sitting outside
Drinking tea
Wrapped in a blanket
And the first hints of sun
I read it
The whole thing
Three times over
I read it and I read it and I read it
Begin finish begin

And I read it now
I should feel bad
For taking it
For taking what isn't mine
But it didn't feel right to leave it
It didn't feel right
And I was already doing
So much wrong
I couldn't bring myself
To add this
One last thing
So I took it
And I read it

Begin finish begin
And I look for answers
And it gives me none
Just tells me
To keep reading

It's raining in the city
Pouring
Pelting
It's raining
And it soothes me
Soothes my skin
Washes away the sweat
Washes away the dirt

It's raining
And I need it
Like I need air
Like I need the blood in my veins
The blood on my tongue
I need it
And it comes to me
And it covers me
Drenches me
And I need it
I need it
I need to be cleaned
I need to forget

I need to start
again

I stand outside our house
For too long
I stand until
The door opens
And Freddie yells
Asking
If I'm done being dramatic yet
And I say no
Five more minutes please
And he scoffs
And slams the door

I stand until the rain stops
Then I go inside

I'm no less dramatic inside
And Freddie makes sure I know it
Henry is pacing
And Freddie is giving me the smallest cookie
A bag of blood is bubbling in the microwave
My favorite mug

Waits in front of me
And I am sitting
Soaking
Tired
I can't hear them
Over the noise in my head
Over the voices
Angry I left
Or angry I came back
It's hard to tell
When they all scream at once
Henry is pacing
Freddie is eating
I am listening

They're loud
They're so loud
They're all I can hear
They roar
Together
They're angry
I think
Relieved
I think
And I'm trying
I am
I'm trying
to listen

And that
That
Surprises them
And they
They
Stop
Surging forwards
Pushing ahead
Filling my head
And that
Surprises
Me

They shrink back
Just a bit
Just a little
But enough
Enough to let me breathe
Enough
To let me listen

Twenty One

I sneak out
And it makes me feel younger than I've ever felt
Maybe younger than I've ever
Let myself feel
I sneak out and I go to
The museum
And I visit them
I visit them all
I stand before them
I let them come to me
Greet me
Talk to me
Talk and talk and talk
And I listen
And I know bits of stories
Snippets of pasts
Pieces of lives
I know how that song makes us feel
And now I know
Why
The woman with the dress
The man with the shield
One by one
I sit on the ground I lean against a wall
I walk I walk I listen I hear
They tell they tell they tell

And I hear and I ask and I wonder
And they tell and they tell and
They tell

I leave them there
I think
Because they are
Quiet
When I leave
Silent when I sneak back in
They whisper
When I bathe and dress for bed
They sing in airy voices when I sleep
And we are quiet
We are quiet

Twenty-Two

I see Claudia again
A week
Or so
Later
I buy her a yellow rose
And I say I am sorry
I am so sorry
And she takes the yellow rose and smiles a bit
And says
And says

Maybe in the next one?

And I smile
And I shrug
And I nod

Maybe
In the next one

It was all built on twigs
I know that
Built up on brittle wood and pebbles
Globs of glue and mounds of hope

It was sheer determination
The taste of loneliness on the back of our tongues
The feel of each other's fingertips
It was built with what we had
It was built with all we had
Built with
Built on
Tired and needy
Heartbeats and kisses and touches and words and
It was built
Tall
And proud
Shaky
But built to last
If it got a little help
If it was always
Patched up
When it cracked
Propped up
When it wavered
Against all odds
It was built to last
And so it did
It did

But I wanted to love right
Be loved right
I wanted to love

Hard
I wanted to be the best at love
At giving
At getting
Taking and spreading and sharing and coveting
I loved with a sharp competitive glint
Bouncing from my every edge
I loved with stubbornness
I loved with a snarl
Quiet inside me
I bit I took I bit I took
And I don't want
To take

So I give her a yellow rose
And I want
I want to say
Please
I want to say
In a voice that isn't mine
Please
Let me tell you I love you
Let me tell you how I love you
How much
How well
How good
How good
How good

Let me tell you
You can forget
If you want
You can blink and let it go
If you want
Just first
Let me tell you
I want
I want

I don't

I give her a yellow rose
She gives me a smile
We cross our fingers behind our backs
And we say goodbye

And the walk home is quiet
The walk home is quiet

AN INTERVIEW WITH AUTHOR MEG GREHAN

Siobhán Parkinson is the author of more than thirty books and was Ireland's first ever Laureate na nÓg (children's laureate). In 2010 she founded Little Island Books. Here Siobhán talks to Meg Grehan about Baby Teeth *and what she is writing next.*

Meg, all your novels are girl/girl love stories written in verse for a young readership. But they are quite different, and this third one branches out quite radically from *The Space Between* and *The Deepest Breath*. Can you tell us a bit about how you came to write this very different novel?

Before I started writing *Baby Teeth* I tried to write a few other projects but nothing was really working. It was during COVID–19 lockdown and I wasn't feeling my best so I decided to just write something for fun. I had the idea for a vampire who lives life after life, I had a clear image of my main character and I just let myself think about it for a couple of months. I started a journal where I wrote all of my ideas and collected photos and art that inspired me. I let it sit in my head and grow and when I felt ready I wrote it in a couple of weeks. It was the most fun I've had writing a book so far!

It's quite different from my first two books, but I think they are all about identity in some way. Beth from *The Space Between* kind of lost her identity and had to rebuild it; Stevie from *The Deepest Breath* was discovering her identity; and Immy is grappling with hers. They're all about big feelings that can be hard to reconcile and they all revolve around some kind of love.

The heroines of *The Space Between* and *The Deepest Breath* are easy for the reader to empathise with: likable characters trying to find their way in the world. The heroine of this book is more complex. Did you set out to create a character that readers might feel ambivalent about?

I didn't set out specifically to make a character people might have mixed feelings toward but I knew that was what the story needed. My first two books wouldn't work if you didn't like Beth or Stevie but this book is different and in a way, kind of liberating. I could write the character exactly how I wanted, knowing her choices might frustrate or anger the reader and knowing that that could work for this story. Immy has a lot to figure out and deal with, but there's a lot of love in her and I hope that comes through.

It seems to me that what you are doing here is taking the trope of the vampire and using it to explore the theme of desire, which might have been more difficult to do in a realistic story. Was that a deliberate choice and did it give you some level of freedom as you wrote?

It did give me some freedom. Everything is heightened by the fact that they're vampires, the stakes are a little higher (excuse the pun). I feel like vampires have this innate drama to them and that let me go further into themes of desire and identity than I would have if they were human.

We get some glimpses of life in the pseudo-family to which Immy belongs and their down-to-earth group dynamic. Were you 'grounding' Immy by making her part of a kind of family?

I love the trope of the "found family" and I've always wanted to write about one. I love characters who choose to love and care for each other. I wanted the reader to see Immy in another light, not just with Claudia. I knew while writing that Immy and her decisions would be polarising so I really wanted to show another side of her, one that is a little softer. I also just love Freddie and Henry a lot so the scenes at home with them were some of my favourites to write.

Baby Teeth obviously comes out of an enthusiasm for horror, though this is not a horror story. Could you tell us a bit about your influences?

I love horror! I'm a very anxious person, I'm scared a lot of the time and of a lot of things. But there's something about the controlled fear that horror brings that I just love. For however long the movie or book lasts I know that I'm supposed to be scared, and there's something comforting about that. I didn't have any solid influences but I did read a lot about the history of vampires, which I loved.

This is your third novel in verse. How did you come to discover your voice as a verse novelist?

I've always loved poetry. I was a drama kid and did lots of poetry competitions, both reciting and writing. When I started writing *The Space Between*, I was writing in prose and while the story felt right, something was off. I decided to give verse a go and I fell completely in love with it. It just comes naturally to me, it's very instinctual, you have to trust your gut and let the words tell you where they want to be. I think it's the most fun way to write. I've grown a lot since my first book, I trust myself more and I just let the book be what it wants to be instead of worrying too much about every word being the exact right one.

There are hints in this story that Immy flits through 'life' on various planes and in various manifestations. It's all a bit mysterious, quite tantalising. Do you have any plans to write about her again, maybe in a different situation?

I would love to write about Immy again, either the Immy we know or one of her past selves. She's such a fun character because she can be anyone. Right now, for fun, I'm writing about what happened when Freddie left, where he went and what he did. I'd also love to write about the time when Henry and Freddie fell in love. It's the first book I've written that I don't feel quite finished with and I see myself exploring this little universe a lot.

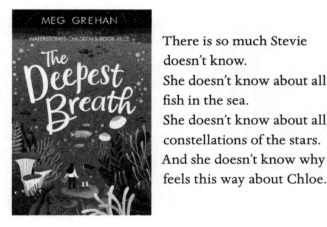

ALSO BY MEG GREHAN

The Space Between

For ages 14+

Winner: Eilís Dillon Award for debut novel at the
Children's Books Ireland Awards 2018

It's New Year's Eve, and Beth plans
to spend a whole year alone, in
her snug, safe house. But she has
reckoned without floppy-eared,
tail-wagging Mouse, who comes
nosing to her window. Followed
shortly by his owner, Alice.

As Beth's year of solitude rolls
out, Alice gently steals her way
first into Beth's house and later
into her heart. And by the time
New Year's Eve comes round again – who knows?

A tender and delicate love story in verse, *The Space
Between* is a tale of how warmth, support and friendship
can overcome mental anguish.

*'A tale of redemption through love; a beguiling read for anyone who
suffers depressive illness, or who wants to understand it better.'*
– The Irish Examiner

*'Pleasantly claustrophobic and deeply atmospheric, this
bowled me over.'* – Gay Community News

Needlework

by Deirdre Sullivan

For ages 14+

Winner: Honour Award for Fiction,
Children's Books Ireland Awards 2017

Ces longs to be a tattoo artist and embroider skin with beautiful images. But for now she's just trying to reach adulthood without falling apart.

Powerful, poetic and disturbing, *Needlework* is a girl's meditation on her efforts to maintain her bodily and spiritual integrity in the face of abuse, violation and neglect.

'Reading *Needlework* is similar to getting your first tattoo – it's searing, often painful, but it is an experience you'll never forget.'
– *Louise O'Neill*

'*Needlework* is a powerful novel that deserves to be read.'
– *Sarah Crossan*

'A novel that is just as sharp and precise as its title suggests.'
– *Doireann Ní Ghríofa*

Tangleweed and Brine

by Deirdre Sullivan
Illustrated by Karen Vaughan

For ages 14+

Winner: Book of the Year,
Children's Books Ireland Awards 2018
Winner: YA Book of the Year, Irish Book Awards 2017
Irish Times Ticket Readers' Choice for YA fiction 2017

A multi-award-winning collection of twelve dark feminist retellings of traditional fairytales from one of Ireland's leading writers for young people. In the tradition of Angela Carter, stories such as Cinderella and Rumpelstiltskin are given a witchy makeover. Intricately illustrated with black and white line drawings.

'An absolute stunner of a book.'
– Claire Hennessy, The Irish Times

'Exquisitely written and powerful –
I'm enchanted by it.' – Marian Keyes

'Beguiling, bewitching and poetic.' – Juno Dawson

Savage Her Reply

by Deirdre Sullivan
Illustrated by Karen Vaughan

For ages 14+

Winner: Book of the Year,
KPMG Children's Books Ireland Awards 2021
Winner: YA Book of the Year, An Post Irish Book Awards 2020

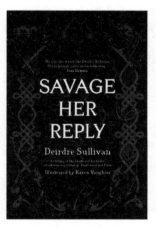

A dark, feminist retelling of Irish fairytale The Children of Lir. Aífe marries Lir, a chieftain with four children by his previous wife. Jealous of his affection for his children, the witch Aífe turns them into swans for 900 years.

Retold through the voice of Aífe, *Savage Her Reply* is unsettling and dark, feminist and fierce, yet nuanced in its exploration of the guilt of a complex character.

'*Saturated with the power of Sullivan's lyrical prose.*'
– *Imogen Russell Williams*, The Guardian

'*Breathes new life into the Irish legend of the Children of Lir.*'
– *Fiona Noble*, The Observer

ABOUT LITTLE ISLAND

Little Island is an independent Irish publisher that looks for the best writing for young readers, in Ireland and internationally. Founded in 2010 by Ireland's inaugural Laureate na nÓg (Children's Laureate), Little Island has published over 100 books, many of which have won awards and been published in translation around the world.

RECENT AWARDS FOR LITTLE ISLAND BOOKS

Book of the Year, KPMG Children's Books Ireland Awards 2021
Savage Her Reply by Deirdre Sullivan

YA Book of the Year, An Post Irish Book Awards 2020
Savage Her Reply by Deirdre Sullivan

Judges' Special Prize, KPMG Children's Books Ireland Awards 2020
The Deepest Breath by Meg Grehan

Shortlisted: The Waterstones Children's Book Prize 2020 (Shortlisted)
The Deepest Breath by Meg Grehan

IBBY Honours List 2020
Mucking About by John Chambers

Children's Book of the Year (Junior), An Post Irish Book Awards 2019
123 Ireland by Aoife Dooley

Literacy Association of Ireland Children's Book Award 2019
Bank by Emma Quigley

Great Reads Award 2019
Dangerous Games by James Butler

Honour Award for Illustration, Children's Books Ireland Awards 2019
Dr Hibernica Finch's Compelling Compendium of Irish Animals by Aga Grandowicz and Rob Maguire

Little Island
Books create waves

www.littleisland.ie